William Leonard Gage, Wilhelm Adolf Lampadius

Life of Felix Mendelssohn Bartholdy

William Leonard Gage, Wilhelm Adolf Lampadius

Life of Felix Mendelssohn Bartholdy

ISBN/EAN: 9783337094515

Printed in Europe, USA, Canada, Australia, Japan

Cover: Foto ©Raphael Reischuk / pixelio.de

More available books at **www.hansebooks.com**

LIFE

OF

FELIX MENDELSSOHN BARTHOLDY.

𝔉rom the 𝔊erman of 𝔚. 𝔄. 𝔏ampadius.

WITH SUPPLEMENTARY SKETCHES

BY

JULIUS BENEDICT, HENRY F. CHORLEY, LUDWIG RELLSTAB,
BAYARD TAYLOR, R. S. WILLIS, AND J. S. DWIGHT.

EDITED AND TRANSLATED

By WILLIAM LEONHARD GAGE.

NEW YORK & PHILADELPHIA:

FREDERICK LEYPOLDT.

BOSTON: S. R. URBINO; NICHOLS & NOYES.

1865.

ALVORD, PRINTER.

TO

JOHN S. DWIGHT,

WHOSE ENTHUSIASTIC ADMIRATION FIRST MADE THE LETTERS OF
MENDELSSOHN ACCESSIBLE TO AMERICAN READERS, AND
WHOSE TASTES ARE SO FULLY IN HARMONY WITH
THE PURITY OF MENDELSSOHN'S
GENIUS AND LIFE,

𝕿𝖍𝖎𝖘 𝕿𝖗𝖆𝖓𝖘𝖑𝖆𝖙𝖎𝖔𝖓 𝖎𝖘 𝕯𝖊𝖉𝖎𝖈𝖆𝖙𝖊𝖉,

AS A SLIGHT EXPRESSION OF THANKS FOR JUDICIOUS COUNSEL
AND TIMELY ENCOURAGEMENT.

EDITOR'S PREFACE.

THE time predicted by one who wrote the sentence years ago seems to have come, "when every line and every word from Mendelssohn's pen would be treasured by the world." Most great composers make their appeal for recognition to a comparatively small circle of admirers, and are rarely quoted beyond the domain of their art. It is so with Mendelssohn neither in Germany, in England, nor in America. Chorley little knew what a weighty sentence he was inditing, when he penned the words, "There may come a day yet, when the example of Mendelssohn's life, yet more than of his works, may be invoked in Germany." In England there was always a passionate adoration of him as a man ; the fascinating presence, the stories of his remarkable culture, his unselfishness, his moral purity, his entirely religious and Christian character, awakening an interest in every thing pertaining to him, which found hardly an exaggerated expression in the pages of

" Charles Auchester," and which has not ceased
yet. And within a few years the people of culture in America have begun to take as deep an
interest in Mendelssohn as those of Germany and
England : hardly any books have found more
enthusiastic readers among us than Mendelssohn's
Letters. That wonderful romance, the most
wholesome gift by far of Miss Sheppard to the
world, " Charles Auchester," has found thousands of admirers, who have been charmed by its
pages. It was the fashion years ago to fling at
that book as rhapsodical ; but this biography will
convince the reader, if the Letters of Mendelssohn
have not already done so, that that work, with all
its splendid coloring, and all its seeming exagge-
rations, scarcely overrated the glory, the beauty,
the capacity, and the compass of Mendelssohn's
life. A completer transcript of the spirit of
Mendelssohn could hardly have been made. His
wonderful reach of memory was certainly not
over-estimated in the scene where he directs the
" Messiah " from his memory of the score : that
would have been a light task for Mendelssohn.
The death of his sister Fanny, narrated in this
biography, is closely adhered to in the romance :
the characters of Zelter, Joachim the violinist,
Jenny Lind, and Sterndale Bennett, are finely
painted in Aronach, Charles Auchester, Julia
Bennett, and Starwood Burney. But it were

needless to speak more at length : enough to say, that, the more we know of Mendelssohn, the more clearly we see how closely Miss Sheppard adhered to the facts and coloring of his life in her fascinating portrait. It is no descent from the Seraphael of "Charles Auchester" to the writer of Mendelssohn's Letters. The plane is the same, though the true Mendelssohn is a shade more joyous and less pensive than the counterfeit. But we trace the same exquisite purity in both; the same unsordid spirit; the same unwillingness to write, except under the stress of a great inspiration; the same freedom from envy; the same recoil from all immorality; the same abhorrence of French and Italian sensuality; the same devotion to what is good, noble, and, in the strictest use of speech, Christ-like.

Not long after the death of Mendelssohn, Lampadius, a friend of his, a musical amateur, and evidently a man of nice tastes and of high-toned character, wrote a biography of the great composer, which has been made the basis of all the smaller sketches of his life, but which now appears in a literal translation from the German for the first time. It may be said of it, that it is not the best biography of Mendelssohn that could be written, but it is the best and indeed the only one that has been written, or is likely to be for some time. Doubtless, the time will come when this brief work will be superseded by one more exhaustive : till then, it remains without a rival. It has, too, some qualities of striking and sterling character; it was written with all the loving ardor which followed Mendelssohn's sudden death; it is a bouquet of fresh flowers laid on his grave. It portrays his career as Director at Leipzig, certainly the best part of his life, with minuteness and fidelity; and in its whole delineation, while it shows unmistakable marks of the warmth of friendship, it yet displays colors vivid, glowing, and delightful. I have preserved all his details; and the record will hardly be judged by musical readers to be too full : for it is a great advantage to know what were just the programmes selected by so consummate a judge as Mendelssohn for performance at those Leipzig Concerts which made that city, while he lived, the musical capital of Europe.

Acting as editor as well as translator, I have sought to bring together all available materials in English, French, and German, which could illustrate Mendelssohn's character and career, and thus render the work of Lampadius even more complete than its author left it. Very much, however, of what has been written, — Neumann's sketch in "Die neuen Componisten," and "Julie de Marguerette's," for instance, — are only Lampadius reproduced in briefer compass. Still, this search has not been inadequately rewarded ; and in the modest and admirable account, by Julius Benedict, of Mendelssohn in England ; in the free, sparkling, and valuable chapters from Chorley's " Modern Music ; " in Rellstab's, Bayard Taylor's, and Richard Storrs Willis's glimpses of Mendelssohn ; in the descriptive analysis of his oratorio " Elijah " by Mr. Dwight, — the reader will find much that will throw light on the subject of this biography as a man and an artist.

Preparing this work as a recreation amid severer studies, I part with it not as freed from a heavy burden, but as turning back from a holiday's pastime to labor. Brief and fragmentary as it is as a biography, it cannot fail to do good if it shall bring any of our American people to know and love the pure spirit of Mendelssohn.

WILLIAM LEONHARD GAGE.

CONTENTS.

CHAPTER I.

VIII.

IX.

X.

XI.

XII.

XIII.

XIV.

XV.

XVI.

APPENDIX.

LIFE OF MENDELSSOHN.

CHAPTER I.

Mendelssohn's Parentage and Birth. — Precocious Talents. — Studies with Zelter. — Zelter's Letters to Goethe regarding Mendelssohn. — He is taken to Paris by his Father to see Cherubini. — Compliments from Goethe. — Mendelssohn visits England. — He visits Goethe. — Goethe's Influence on the Musician's whole Career. — He becomes Moscheles' Pupil. — "Midsummer Night's Dream" Overture. — He studies at Berlin University. — Preparations to travel.

WHEN a citizen dies whose life has been devoted to the common weal, his city mourns his loss with a general grief; when a ruler who has been devoted to all the duties of his office goes to his grave, his countrymen lament over his death: but, when a king in the domain of genius is withdrawn from the sphere of his labors, thousands upon thousands of hearts which beat with love for what is good and true are filled with sorrow, thousands upon thousands of eyes are filled with tears. Such sorrow is that which laments the premature death of FELIX MENDELSSOHN BARTHOLDY, who, had he lived, would now (1864) be but at the age when most men are in the very prime of their years. For in him departed the last classic spirit of Germany's great epoch of culture. But as Providence blessed him in life, giving him no harder battle to fight than that which came from the constantly unsatisfied aspirations struggling within his own breast; even so, in his death, the gain is with him, and not with us. Not because he took his departure after having attained the highest summit of his fame, (for who is bold enough to insist, that, if he had lived, he would have produced something greater than he ever did?) but because he, though a classic, is honored at a time when Germany has ceased to honor its greatest spirits as it ought; when a Beethoven, a Mozart, a Schiller, have to wait, and as yet in vain, for one to rise, and show the world the wealth of their genius and the course of their lives.

Felix Mendelssohn Bartholdy, son of Abraham Mendelssohn, a well-known banker, and himself a man of very refined tastes, and grandson of Moses Mendelssohn, the eminent philosopher, first saw the light in Hamburg the 3d of February, 1809. The house in which he was born was the large one, still standing, just back of St. Michael's Church; and in the same house, by a happy coincidence, his warm friend and fellow-artist, Ferdinand David, was born just a year later. He was the second of four children,— Fanny, the oldest; then Felix, Paul, and Rebecca. His mother, born a Bartholdy, was a very gifted woman, and watched over the progress of the boy with devoted love, which was requited by the

utmost affection. The father, too, was always regarded
with great tenderness by Felix. When the child was
three or four years old, the family removed to Berlin.
Under the favoring star which held him back, from his
birth, from all contact with what was common and vul-
gar, his wonderful talents opened and ripened early.
Even in his eighth year, he played the piano with
remarkable facility; and at the same early age he dis-
closed that remarkable power of criticism, that lynx-eye
as Zelter termed it, which enabled him to detect six
consecutive fifths in a piece of Sebastian Bach, which
escaped the keen eye of Zelter himself; and also that
almost miraculous fineness of ear, which in the most
powerful orchestra, or in an immense chorus, detected
the least error of a single instrument or of a voice.
He showed, too, an uncommon productivity for his years.
Zelter, the veteran in musical science, and Ludwig Berger, the master in musical art, were his first teachers
in composition and in piano-forte playing. Zelter called
Mendelssohn his best scholar, even at the age of twelve;
and his letters to Goethe are evidences of his warm
interest in the lad, although that interest was often
disguised by a rough address, which doubtless did some
injury to the gentle spirit of young Felix. The best
fruit of this correspondence was the intimate relation in
which after this he always stood to Goethe. This near-
ness, and ease of approach, to a nature so grand and rich

as Goethe's, was a very great advantage to Mendelssohn, and tended to encourage all that was large, generous, and noble in him, and to repress all that was small, contracted, and sickly. It would be a great treat* to the reading-world to be permitted to look into the correspondence of Goethe and Mendelssohn: for the present, it is enough to glean from Zelter's and Goethe's letters the progress of this always-increasing intimacy. Zelter speaks of Felix in expressions like these: "He plays the clavichord like a young devil;" or, "Felix is always the first." And, in the autumn of 1821, he writes to Goethe regarding a visit which he was about to make him: "I want my Doris and my best scholar to look upon your face before I die." In November of that year, he brought together his aged friend and his loved pupil. Afterward Goethe wrote to Zelter, in his cool, measured way, "Say a good word to Felix too, and his parents. Since he went away, my piano has been dumb: an effort to waken it again would, I am afraid, be useless after that." But this casual interest was destined to be yet deepened. Zelter wrote more fully regarding his boy's wonderful talents and great industry, and Goethe's friendship grew warmer towards him. On the 8th of February, 1824, Zelter wrote, "Yesterday evening, Felix's fourth opera was brought out here in a little circle of us, with the dialogue. There are

* Happily granted now (1864).

three acts, which, with the two ballets, occupied about two hours and a half. The work was received with much applause. I can hardly master my own wonder how the boy, who is only about fifteen, has made such progress. Everywhere you find what is new, beautiful, and peculiar, — wholly peculiar. 'Tis massive, as if from an experienced hand; the orchestra interesting, not oppressive, not wearisome, — not mere accompaniment. The performers like to play it; yet it is not very easy. What is known comes and goes, not as if taken for granted, but as if welcome, and just in its appropriate place, — life, joy without impatient haste, tenderness, grace, love, passion, innocence. The overture is a wonderful thing. You seem to see a painter rubbing a dingy color with brush and finger on the canvas, till at last a finished group emerges. You are amazed: you look to see how it came about, and only see that it must be so because it is true."

In this rather rough and disjointed yet expressive style, Zelter shows the gradual emerging of some central theme, around which a group of musical fancies arrange themselves; just as is the case, for example, in the overture, "The Hebrides." — "Certainly," Zelter goes on to say, "I speak as a grandfather who pardons his boy. I know what I say, and I have said nothing that I cannot prove. First the multitude applauded; then the orchestra-people and the singers: and that is the way

2

by which you can tell whether a piece is received warmly or coldly; whether the applause is real and generous, or only affected. This is a thing for you to notice. When the performer enters with his soul into what lies before him, and testifies that the composer has suited him, that is true applause; that tells the whole." How this wise word of Zelter's was confirmed afterwards! How enthusiastically the singers and players of Leipzig, for example, attended the rehearsals of " St. Paul " and the " Hymn of Praise" at a later day! How unwearied the orchestra was in overcoming all the technical difficulties which the overture and the music of the " Midsummer Night's Dream " presented! No one realized how, by pleasantry and earnestness, by appropriate praise and rightly directed blame, by his quiet glance and undemonstrative yet effective manner, he was able to help the performers over all the hard passages.

The following year (1825), Mendelssohn's father took him to Paris to introduce him to Cherubini, and to inquire of that distinguished musician, with a modesty creditable to both father and son, whether Felix had such a decided musical talent as would justify his devoting himself exclusively to that department of art.* Cherubini's answer was, of course, in the affirmative.

* Mendelssohn supported the great violinist Baillot, at this time, in his quartet in B minor.

On their return, they both visited Goethe. The latter wrote to Zelter, under date May 21, 1825: "Felix produced his new quartet to the amazement of every one. This personal dedication to me, through the ear, has pleased me very much." In June, he sent to the young Mendelssohn what Zelter called "a pretty love-letter." Mendelssohn reciprocated the compliment by sending to Goethe the next year a carefully elaborated copy of Terence's "Andria." In a letter written Oct. 11, 1826, Goethe bade Zelter thank Felix for "this very skilful specimen of earnest æsthetic studies: his work will be a lasting fund of entertainment to the Weimar scholars these long winter evenings." In April, 1829, Mendelssohn went to England at Moscheles' invitation; and, while riding out in a gig with a friend, he was unfortunately thrown out, and severely injured in the knee. After Goethe had heard of this from Zelter, he wrote with the most anxious interest: "I wish also to learn whether good news has come about our excellent Felix. I take the greatest interest in him; for it is painful in the extreme to see one, of whom so much is expected, put in peril by such an occurrence. Tell me something cheering about him."

But the gifted young composer received his real dedication to art, during a fortnight's visit to Goethe, just before his journey to Italy. What a sweet foretaste of the pleasures he was about to enjoy, what a delightful promise of what was in store, did the young Mendelssohn receive from him who sang the song of the "Land wo die Citronen blühn"! How much satisfaction Goethe derived from that visit, we learn from his letter to Zelter, under date of June 3: "Just now, this early summer morning, under a beautiful sky, Felix has taken his departure with Ottilie (Madame von Goethe), Ulrike (Fräulein Poggwisch), and the children (among them Walter von Goethe, the present composer), after spending a fortnight with us, delighting us with his art, and leaving with us the memory of delightful hours. His visit will indeed be a cherished thing. To me his presence was especially valuable, as I found my relations to music still unchanged. I listened with satisfaction and delight. The historical development of music, as Felix portrayed it, was particularly interesting; for who can understand a thing who does not penetrate it far enough to know its history? The chief excellence in Felix is, that he not only thoroughly understands the history of musical science, but his rare memory brings to him the best pieces of each era, and enables him to play at will what best illustrates the development of music. From Bach down, he has called Haydn, Mozart, and Gluck back to life. Of the great moderns he has given examples enough; and, lastly, he has played his own pieces in such a way as to make me both feel and remember

them. He has gone from here with my heartiest bless-
ings. Remember me very cordially to his parents."
After this time, up to Goethe's death, the two remained
in constant correspondence; and Goethe always expressed his admiration of his "cheerful, affectionate,
most interesting letters," as well as took the most active
interest in his progress. On the 4th of January, 1831,
he writes to Zelter: " Felix, whose welfare and happy
stay in Rome you announce to me, must be always
taken the best care of: such extraordinary talents
joined to such an amiable nature!" On the 31st of
March, he writes : " First of all, I must tell you that I
have just received a very full and affectionate letter
from Felix, which gives me an excellent picture of his
life. There is now no reason to fear that he will go
through fire and water, only to come out at barbarism
at last." How truly this prophecy was fulfilled ! With
what energy Mendelssohn has persevered in all the
decay of art, and amid the rank growth that covers
the glorious old ruins, keeping close only to what was
classic, and in no one of his creations catering to the
depraved taste of the times !

I speak more fully regarding this connection between
Mendelssohn and Goethe than I should, had not this
important step in his progress been overlooked by
most who have lately written about him. He may be
regarded as the last gift of that great period in which

Germany's men of genius tempered their gifts in the furnace of a glorious antiquity; and to show Mendelssohn just his place, and leave upon him an impress so strong that it could never be lost, this connection with Goethe was needed, who united so finely a Greek nature and culture with a genuine German spirit. But, in order to appreciate this connection and its influence, we must review the events in the life of the young artist. I will therefore run through the story of the development of his genius, beginning at the point where we left the lad under the care of Zelter and Ludwig Berger.

Ludwig Berger had planted the young tree: Zelter had tilled the ground around it, and had been a kind of stormy wind to it, shaking it roughly, but only to cause it to sink its roots deeper and stronger. There was wanting, however, even yet, the skilful gardener, combining thoroughness with grace, who should protect it from the frost, and bring its first-fruits to perfection. He was found, in 1824, in Moscheles, an artist of the highest order, whose efforts to bring out the genius of Mendelssohn were crowned with a success which the gifted pupil was the first to ascribe to its right source. I will extract a passage from Moscheles' journal made at that time, which he has kindly permitted me to use, and which will clearly show the relation he then bore to Mendelssohn. "In the autumn of 1824, I gave my first concerts in Berlin. I was acquainted with the Mendelssohn Family, and was soon on terms of intimacy with them. In the course of my daily visits at their house, I became familiar with the musical powers of young Felix, and was much interested in his charming character. His youthful efforts were, to my mind, a sufficient guaranty of the eminence which he was destined to attain. His parents often urged me to give him instruction on the piano; and although his former instructor, Ludwig Berger, consented to this arrangement willingly, yet I hesitated about putting this powerful genius under a leading influence which might have the injurious effect of conflicting with the direction which his own original nature might suggest to him. Yet, at their repeated requests, I did give him lessons. He even then could play any thing that I could, and grasped the slightest hint with lightning-like rapidity. My 'E-flat Major Concerto' he played almost at first sight; and my 'Sonate mélancholique' he rendered very finely." Other passages indicate very pleasantly the intensely musical life of the Mendelssohn household. On the 14th of November, Moscheles was there: it was the celebration of the birthday of his oldest sister, Fanny. A symphony by Mendelssohn was given. He himself played Mozart's " C-minor Concerto;" and, with his sister, a duo-concerto in E major, composed by himself. Zelter and many members of the Royal

Chapel were present. On the 28th of the same month, there was another musical entertainment at the same place, — Mendelssohn's father's house. A symphony in D major by the young artist was given. He played his piano-quartet in C minor; and his sister Fanny, a concerto by Sebastian Bach. On the 5th of December, Mozart's "Requiem" was given. Mendelssohn accompanied on the piano. On the 12th of December, at a similar concert, Felix played his "F-minor Quartet;" and Moscheles gave for the first time his piece, afterwards so famous, — "Homage to Handel." Soon after this, if I mistake not, Moscheles went to England.

The 19th of November, 1826, was a memorable epoch in Mendelssohn's career; for then he played, for the first time, his overture to the "Midsummer Night's Dream," — his first work which bore the distinct marks of genius, and which gave him at once a name in the musical world. He first played it with his sister Fanny, as a duet for the piano.

This is enough to indicate the strong musical direction of his father's household, and to show that Mendelssohn himself furnished the most valuable material, and yet constantly nourished his own genius at the same feast which was so delightful to others. So far as Moscheles' influence on him is concerned, we shall hardly mistake, I suppose, if we set it down as certain, that he confined himself to merely giving him a strong impulse, and hints as to execution ; and yet it is certain that to those hints may be largely ascribed that elegance and roundness, which, with other prominent excellences, were always observable in Mendelssohn's piano-playing, down to the last. Yet Moscheles soon exchanged the relation of teacher for that of friend, — a bond which was always rich in usefulness and real joy to Mendelssohn. It was Moscheles who first introduced him to the great world, by persuading him to come to London ; for it can hardly be denied that the reputation of Mendelssohn first became appreciable in Germany after his return from England. In the place of his youth, in Berlin, his talents did not gain prompt recognition. During all the denial of his genius by this city, Moscheles kept up his courage; and, for this, Mendelssohn remained grateful to the end of his life. There was no lack of letters between them; and from one of Mendelssohn's I make a brief extract. It seems to have been written about 1839. " You still keep up your encouraging words, and show your good-will ; and, so long as *you* do, all the *dii minorum gentium* may make faces as much as they will." All through Mendelssohn's life, he was proud to call himself Moscheles' scholar.

Felix's body and mind were assiduously cared for by his excellent father; trained harmoniously, and not sac-

rificed to the love of music alone. We see him, in his
seventeenth year, devoting himself to gymnastics, riding, and swimming. Having an excellent classical preparation, in 1827 he entered the University of Berlin,
and gave himself earnestly to the cultivation of those
sciences which accorded with his own chosen profession.
Among other professors, he listened to Hegel, who set
great value on music (as Zelter himself tells us); and
soon knew how to reproduce all his peculiarities in a
very pleasant and naïve way. The abstract nature of
Hegel, his dragging every thing practical, every thing
that lay before him, into his system, and his dry, absent way, were a great source of merriment to Felix.
About this time, he went to Stettin to help bring out
there his newest works. On the 11th of March, he
directed Bach's " Passion," which he had practised with
Zelter : for a director of twenty, certainly an amazing
feat.

As early as 1827, Mendelssohn's father had written
to Moscheles, in London, to inquire whether he would
advise Felix to travel. It is probable that he favored
the plan ; yet the father preferred to postpone his son's
departure till the completion of his studies at the university. It was the spring of 1829, when the moment
arrived for the young man to try his pinions in flight
out into the great world. Before we follow him, let us
glance at his productive activity thus far. Mendelssohn

had composed up to this time, so far as I can learn, three quartets, in C minor, F minor, and B minor, for piano, violin, viola, and violoncello ; two sonatas, — one for the piano-forte and violin (F minor), the other for the piano-forte alone (B-flat major) ; a symphony in C minor, and another in D major ; a symphony overture ; various operettas, — among them, the one now printed, " Camacho's Wedding ; " two sets of songs, twelve in each set ; and the two great overtures, — to the " Midsummer Night's Dream," and " A Calm at Sea (*Meeresstille*) and Prosperous Voyage ; " which last he seems to have written soon after the " Midsummer Night's Dream " was finished. If he really composed that overture before viewing the sea, it was as great an effort of the imagination as the picture of Alpine scenery in Schiller's " William Tell." It were not possible for the depressing calm, the joy over the first puffs of air, the sailing of the ship into port, to be better painted by music. Besides these, he composed a capriccio, and some smaller piano pieces, and the octet. But this is enough to show that the young artist displayed a wonderfully precocious genius, and justified the fond hopes which were cherished of his future.

CHAPTER II.

Mendelssohn visits England. — Concerts in London with Sontag. — First public Performance ever given of the " Midsummer Night's Dream " Overture. — He visits Scotland and the Hebrides. — He returns to Germany, visits Munich, and then sets his Steps towards Italy. — His Sojourn in Italy, and its Fruits. — He visits Paris ; thence goes to London ; afterwards, Home to Berlin.

ON the 26th of March, 1829, Mendelssohn informed Moscheles of his bringing out Bach's " Passion Music," and announced his speedy departure. On the 20th of April, he arrived at London. Moscheles had made the directors of the Philharmonic Society acquainted with his extraordinary talents, and prepared every thing for his favorable reception. Mendelssohn brought his old teacher, in manuscript, a sacred cantata on a choral in A minor, a motet for sixteen voices, and his first stringed quartet in A minor. At the Philharmonic Concert, his overture to the " Midsummer Night's Dream " was given publicly for the first time, and pleased very much. At a concert given by Henrietta Sontag, his concerto in E major for two pianos, and his Midsummer overture, were given with the most enthusiastic applause. The journey to Scotland, which he took for his pleasure, suggested to him the over- ture, "Fingal's Cave" or "The Hebrides." He wrote this probably after his return to Berlin the same year. It is said that this was the manner in which the overture, "The Hebrides," took its rise : Men- delssohn's sisters asked him to tell them something about the Hebrides. "It cannot be told, only played," he said. No sooner spoken than he seated himself at the piano, and played the theme which afterwards grew into the overture.

In May, 1830, he continued his travels. At Weimar, as has been already said, he tarried a couple of weeks with Goethe, and thence went to Munich. Here he heard for the first time the eminent pianist, Delphine von Schauroth ; who seems to have inspired Mendelssohn with even more than artistic interest. It is said that the beautiful "Travel Song" from Opus 19, "Bring the Heart's Truest Greeting," which he composed at Rome, is to be ascribed to that interest. He journeyed through Italy in company with several painters, — Hildebrand, Sohn, Hübner, Bendemann, and others ; and arrived at Rome the 1st of November, where he tarried till April, 1831, and thence went to Naples. In Rome, he com- posed the music to Goethe's "First Walpurgis Night;" as if he wanted to free himself, by its bracing vigor, from the untoning influence of the South. It would be interesting to know more about Mendelssohn's stay in Italy.*

He wished much to visit Sicily; but did not, in consequence of his father's wish. On his return from Italy, he visited Switzerland; and in February, 1832, we find him in Paris, where he gave in public his overture to the "Midsummer Night's Dream." It was the third, and, so far as I know, the last time that he visited Paris. The French nature did not please him. After overcoming an attack of cholera in Paris, he went to London. Here he added to the list of his influential friends Klingemann, who was then attached to the Hanoverian embassy, and who wrote the verses to a number of songs by him. This time he could show Moscheles the manuscripts of three new pieces of the highest value, — the music of the "Walpurgis Night," the overture, "Fingal's Cave," and the "G-minor Concerto;" that masterly composition for the piano-forte and orchestra, which will always remain as a fine type of the blended grace, imagination, and fire in Mendelssohn's genius. On the 14th of May, the overture, "Fingal's Cave," was given for the first time at the Philharmonic Concert in London. On the 28th of May, Mendelssohn himself played his "G-minor Concerto" for the first time. The 1st of June, he played, with Moscheles, Mozart's duo-concerto, and di-

---

* This want has been richly supplied in Mendelssohn's Letters from Italy and Switzerland. Philadelphia: F. Leypoldt.

rected the " Midsummer Night's Dream " overture. On the 10th of June, he played fugue music on the organ in St. Paul's Church, to the amazement of all the listeners. He also took part in other entertainments, to all of which I hardly need refer; and, on the 23d of June, he turned his steps towards Berlin.

CHAPTER III.

THE directorship of the Berlin Sing-Academie was
now vacant; and, at the urgent solicitation of his
friends, Mendelssohn applied for the place, as he now
wished for some stated field of labor. He was not elect-
ed, however: the choice fell on Rungenhagen.* By a
series of concerts, whose proceeds were to be applied
to benevolent purposes, Mendelssohn tried to educate
the musical taste of the city. In a round of miscella-
neous duties, and without any definite occupation, he
labored on for some time, till, in the spring of 1833,
he was invited to assume the direction of the annual
Musical Festival at Düsseldorf.

With his visit to Düsseldorf begins a new epoch in
the life of Mendelssohn. The first stage in his career

---

* The opposition seems to have been headed by the more elderly
ladies of the Sing-Academie, though the failure of " Camacho's Wedding " seems to have left a lasting prejudice against Mendelssohn.

was his boyhood in his father's house; the second was the time devoted to travel; and this, to which we now come, was the third, — the one which was to put his genius, power, and learning to the test.

He entered upon his course with a conqueror's tread; gaining an assured success so far as he went, yet in such a way and against such opposition as showed him that he must contend for every inch of his progress. Even among musicians, he found hostile spirits who stood in his path. Yet it was a glorious piece of good fortune that his first invitation carried him to Düsseldorf; for here he rejoined that company of painters with whom he had made the tour of Italy. That whole circle (William Schadow, the sculptor, being the central figure) gave him a most cordial welcome, and not only then, but to the end of his life, remained attached to him in bonds of almost fraternal affection.

But, before we accompany Mendelssohn to this new field of labor, we must follow him to London; and although the direction of the Musical Festival at Düsseldorf falls between a first and second visit to London in 1833, we must enter a little into detail about his reception at that great metropolis. He arrived in London on the 25th of April; and, in conjunction with Moscheles, he composed in two days the four-handed variations on the Gypsy March from " Preciosa," which the two artists played at Moscheles' concert on the 1st of May. This

union of labor went so far, that they sometimes improvised at the same piano, in four-handed playing; demanding a most intimate understanding of each other's
thoughts and feelings in the working-out of the theme.
On the 13th of May, at the Philharmonic Concert, the
symphony in A major, by Mendelssohn, was given; on
the 15th, the variations from " Preciosa;" after which
Mendelssohn left London for Düsseldorf. On the 8th of
June, however, he returned to London in company with
his father. On the 10th of June, an overture in C
major, written by him, was given; probably the same
which had been played at Düsseldorf. For a number
of weeks, the father was confined to his room by lameness. While Felix tended him, he wrote for Moscheles
a four-handed arrangement of his septet. During
these weeks of confinement, he also played to Moscheles,
from manuscript, his overture to " Melusina." It grew
out of a picture which he had probably seen at Düsseldorf, where Melusina appears hovering on the top of a
tower.* Moscheles produced it at the Philharmonic
Concert of April 7, 1834; where, however, it did not
meet with a hearty recognition. Given again in one of
Moscheles' own concerts, in conjunction with a rondo by
Mendelssohn in E-flat major (Op. 29), it was well received. It would have gone better the first time, I

---

* Mendelssohn, in his "Letters," gives quite a different account
of it.

think, had it not been for the weight of the orchestra:
the delicate and unusual style demanded a more gentle
manner of instrumentation. A letter of Mendelssohn
to Moscheles now existing is very interesting, written
after he had received from the latter an account of the
first performance. He thanks him in the heartiest manner, and expresses the highest gratification that the
overture pleased him. Mendelssohn needed a good
deal of approbation at this time to give him confidence
enough in himself, which was wanting as yet. He then
jokingly adds, that Moscheles' praise is better than
three orders of nobility; and goes on to give some
excellent hints about the execution of the piece, — about
the wind-instrumentation, for example, — which he
wanted played *pp;* but he is careful to say not *ppp*
(so strong was his objection to every thing forced and
unnatural). On the 25th of August, 1833, he left London, and did not see it again for a long time.

We now turn back to Düsseldorf. At the great
Musical Festival there, which he directed, and which was
held about the last of May or first of June, the great
overture in C major, written, I think, in 1823 or 1824,
but never performed in Germany till then, was given together with "Israel in Egypt," the great "Leonora" overture in C, the "Pastoral Symphony," Wolf's "Easter
Cantata," and Winter's "Power of Music." He himself played Von Weber's concert-piece. The festival,

honored by the co-operation of the great soloist Madame Decker, was characterized by so admirable a selection, and so excellent a performance, that there was a strong wish to retain the director at Düsseldorf. For this purpose, the city created the office of Municipal Musical Director; assigning him the care of the weekly meetings of the Vocal Society, the care of the Winter Concerts, and the direction of the music in the Catholic church. The concerts seem not to have given all the satisfaction which was hoped; since in the whole time, from November, 1833, to May, 1834, only three were held. Yet no blame can be attached to Mendelssohn, who selected very fine programmes, and twice played the piano himself.

During this period, he was united by ties of the closest intimacy to the poet Immermann. They had known each other before. At Mendelssohn's request, Immermann had written a libretto, in the spring of 1833, from Shakspeare's "Tempest," for Mendelssohn to set to music; but the latter had not found it available. It was interesting; in some passages, highly poetic; but not suitable for opera, as Immermann had a special lack of lyrical talent. This rejection of the libretto had, however, no effect on their friendly relations to each other. These grew more close and intimate; and Immermann seems to have clung to Mendelssohn with the most devoted attachment.

The close friendship of these two distinguished men,

and the low estate to which the German theatre had fallen, inspired the hope that they would effect an entire reformation of the drama. Immermann, Mendelssohn, and Uechtritz, an eminent friend of both, declared themselves ready to enter upon this much-needed work. In the spring of 1834, the preliminary trials were made to test the chances of success. Among them were given "Don Juan" and the "Water-carrier," the first operas which Mendelssohn publicly directed; also Goethe's "Egmont," with Beethoven's music. In the preparation of Calderon's "Steadfast Prince," Mendelssohn composed the following music needed for its representation, — two choruses, a march, a battle-piece, and the melodramatic part. This very interesting and characteristic music has not been used since. These preliminary efforts were so successful, that a company was formed, a large capital raised, and a new and commodious theatre erected, at Düsseldorf. A directory of eleven persons controlled the whole management. Immermann and Mendelssohn were conjoined with them, — the one having the chief direction of the drama; the other, of the opera. As Mendelssohn could not and would not devote himself wholly to this enterprise, he invited to Düsseldorf a friend of his youth, and one of his most skilful scholars, — Julius Rietz. They had been acquainted in Berlin; were of about the same age (Rietz a little the younger); and

Mendelssohn had given him lessons on the piano. I use the title of scholar of Mendelssohn, with regard to Rietz, with no other significance than as denoting one of the best living representatives of the Mendelssohn school, of which there is needed no better specimen than his noble " Festival Overture in A Major." On the 28th of October, 1834, the theatre was opened with the " Prince of Hamburg," and an excellent prologue written by Immermann. At the close of the prologue, Raphael's " Parnassus" was presented as a *tableau vivant,* for which Mendelssohn had composed music.

Unhappily the theatre was a source of misunderstanding between Immermann and Mendelssohn. They both had the best, the noblest of intentions: they only lacked the requisite theatrical experience. Mendelssohn gave offence by bringing from Berlin some young and unripe performers. Immermann, on the other hand, wanted to exalt the spoken drama at the expense of the opera; or, rather, he wanted no opera at all. This gave rise to reproaches on both sides, an exchange of sharp words, and, at last, to total estrangement. Mendelssohn withdrew, after he had studied and twice directed "Oberon," in the very first weeks of the first season, and despite his own engagement; and his relation to Immermann was never again one of friendship. The theatre sustained itself with great difficulty till the spring of 1837.

But though his tie to a great poet was thus dissolved, yet his relations to the painters of Düsseldorf grew closer than ever. He himself cultivated in those years his remarkable powers in drawing; and under the direction of Schirmer, the great landscape painter of Düsseldorf, to whom he afterwards dedicated his CXIV. Psalm, executed a very beautiful sketch in water-colors. He exercised this gift in a very attractive manner in adorning the albums of his friends. To Klingemann in London, for instance, he sent an album containing thirty drawings, illustrating Klingemann's own poems. Prof. Moscheles also possesses a number of sketches from his hand, pleasant reminiscences of their artist-life together, with exquisite touches of humor where they illustrate Moscheles as a musician.

Meantime, in the winter of 1834–5, the concerts, and the weekly meetings of the Vocal-music Society, were in their perfect bloom. There were seven concerts given, at two of which the "Messiah" and Haydn's "Seasons" were performed. But the great business of Mendelssohn at Düsseldorf was the composition of "St. Paul." Besides that great and enduring work of genius, he wrote the three piano capriccios (Op. 33); a number of songs without words; among others, those of the second set, and the three Heine songs in the first set of his four-part songs (Op. 41). In all sorts of musical delights, he was not wanting; and Mendelssohn was not at all chary in playing for the entertainment of his friends.

In the spring of 1835, he was invited to take the direction of the Cologne Musical Festival; which he did. There were given: " Festival Overture," by Beethoven, in C; Handel's " Solomon," with new organ part by Mendelssohn; Beethoven's " Eighth Symphony;" Milton's " Morning Song," with Reichardt's music; "Overture to Euryanthe," and a " Religious March and Hymn" by Cherubini. The gratification of the Cologne musical public was complete. In token of their appreciation, the committee presented him with the London edition of Handel's Works, and their thanks beautifully written on parchment, together with the signatures of the six hundred performers whom he had directed.

Meantime, Mendelssohn's reputation had reached Leipzig, and there was a strong wish to secure his services in that city. Some of the most eminent fellows of the university had cherished the hope of accomplishing the object by founding a professorship of music for Mendelssohn, whose thorough mastery of musical science was known to them. He was questioned regarding this. He wrote back, politely thanking them for the honor, but declining to read lectures, for which, as we all learned afterwards, he had no talent. Meantime, the wish to secure him had grown into a determination; and the very hand which wrote to him about a professorship was instrumental in procuring for him the direction of the Leipzig Gewandhaus concerts. This post he accepted. According to his Düsseldorf contract, he could be released from his engagement there at the end of two years. He obtained this release; and after giving, on the 2d of July, 1835, a very choice concert, — in which he played his piano capriccio in B minor, — he left Düsseldorf, to the great grief of a large circle of friends.

CHAPTER IV.

Mendelssohn becomes the Director of the Gewandhaus Concerts at Leipzig. —
His strict Training of the Orchestra. — His Efforts to educate a refined Taste
for Classical Music. — His first Appearance with the Bâton.— The Concerts
under his Direction. — Ferdinand David comes to Leipzig.

WITH his coming to Leipzig (which was his home
from September, 1835, to 1844, and from 1845
to the end of his life), begins the fourth period of his
career, — an epoch full of the richest, most varied, most
untiring activity for himself, and one of such splendor
in the musical life of Leipzig as can hardly be expected
to come again.   He directed the Gewandhaus concerts
personally from 1835 to 1841; producing during this
time a great number of master-pieces of enduring excellence, yet compelled to earn his way into public favor
step by step.   He knew how to command the resources
of the place perfectly in orchestra, dilettanti, and chorus
singers; to bear with them with the greatest patience;
to stimulate them all into activity; and thus to obtain
effects almost unequalled until then.   For he did not
confine himself to the almost purely classical training
necessary for the Gewandhaus concerts, but improved
every opportunity to influence the public taste; so that

it may be truly said, that, in the practice of one art, he developed an appreciation of all, and gave to the life of the cultivated people of Leipzig a higher ideal by the pure moral and truly æsthetic influence which he exercised over them. He did this not only by an always admirable selection of the music to be performed at the concerts, but also by awakening, through his superb direction of the orchestra, a taste on the part of the public for the works of the later great masters ; as, for example, the " Ninth Symphony " of Beethoven. He not only cultivated a relish for the historical development of music, but he summoned the mighty spirits of the past to the help and delight of the present age, and often combined the entire musical resources of Leipzig in rendering some of their master-pieces. We leave this general sketch of his influence in that city, to enter a little upon some of the details of his life there.

The 4th of October, 1835, was an eventful day for the musical history of Leipzig ; for, on that day, Mendelssohn assumed the direction of the Gewandhaus concerts. " On his appearance," we find in a record of the concert, published in a musical journal, "the murmur of applause which ran . through the crowded audience testified to the welcome which Leipzig gave him. The universal favorite, Mendelssohn's overture, ' A Calm at Sea and a Happy Voyage,' (*Meeresstille, &c.*) was given as gently and gracefully as the public expected from a

director so skilful at the opening of his course with us."
It may be interesting to many readers to know what other
pieces were also given on this occasion.   There were a
scena and aria in E major by Weber, Spohr's " Violin
Concerto, No. 11," Introduction to Cherubini's " Ali
Baba;" and, for the second part, Beethoven's " B-flat
Major Symphony," which was given with a precision till
then unknown in Leipzig.   Mendelssohn had carefully
studied the piece, and directed it in person,—an arrangement new to us, but of eminent propriety.   There had
been no lack of excellence in former days, when the con-
cert-master and the first violin had the direction of
Beethoven's symphonies; yet of that nice shading, that
exact adaptation of each instrument, that perfect harmony of all instruments, attained under Mendelssohn's
direction, there had been no conception.   The performance of the " B-flat Symphony " — that ethereal, soul-
ful music — was one of the master effects gained by
Mendelssohn as a director.   Every new rendering threw
new light upon it; so that the listeners were compelled
to say, " So perfectly performed we never heard it before."   It was given the last time under his direction in
the winter of 1846–7.

On the 9th of October, Moscheles, who had come to
Leipzig (perhaps on Mendelssohn's invitation), gave a
concert, which was crowded, in which he played his
" Hommage à Haendel," and at which the overture,

" The Hebrides " was given. At the second subscription
concert, Mozart's " E-flat Major Symphony " was played
more beautifully than ever at Leipzig before. At the
fourth subscription concert, Mendelssohn played his own
noble " G-minor Concerto." He was received at the
very outset with applause ; which strengthened, however,
with every movement, as the admiration increased at
the ease, elegance, and grace of his playing. Mendelssohn's loyalty towards the great musical classics
appeared in a manner very grateful to the audience,
when, in the fifth concert, he brought out Haydn's
" Symphony, No. 4." The sixth concert was thoroughly
classic, — Gluck's overture to " Iphigenia in Aulis ; " an
aria from Paer, with violin obligato ; chorus and first
finale from " Titus," and Beethoven's " Heroic Symphony." This auspicious opening was sadly interrupted,
towards the end of November, by the death of Mendelssohn's father. The son mourned deeply over his
loss, which was indeed a very severe one, as those who
now know the father through his letters to his son are
aware.

About this time, Mendelssohn renewed his intimacy
with a friend of his childhood, — Ferdinand David,
afterwards so well known, not merely to the Leipzig
public, but to the musical world. Born in the same
house with Mendelssohn, he had early lost his parents ;
and had been taken under the guardianship of the elder

Mendelssohn, and educated mainly in his family. The talents of the two boys expanded side by side. David had adopted the violin, and had early manifested wonderful skill on that instrument. He first tried his fortune in Hamburg, his native city; but soon turned back to Berlin, and first found a recognition in the Royal Theatre, where his playing won great regard. An invitation from a gentleman of high position in Dorpat drew him next to that place. After being separated from each other many years, the friends met at the family mansion in Berlin. It was a most happy incident for Mendelssohn to meet such a friend at such a time. They joined their fortunes, and turned back to Leipzig, to be associated till death sundered the bond. David entered upon a brilliant career as a violinist there, and always stood shoulder to shoulder with his friend in the furtherance of all his plans.

CHAPTER V.

Mendelssohn finishes his "St. Paul." — Its first Performance. — Changes in
the Work. — He directs a Festival at Frankfort. — Enjoyment in that City. —
Meets his future Wife. — Tribute to her Memory. — Sea-bathing. — Returns
to his Place at Leipzig. — Concerts there. — Mendelssohn as a Director. —
Pleasant Surprise at one of the Concerts. — William Sterndale Bennett
visits Leipzig. — "St. Paul" sung there. — Brilliant Effect of the Work. —
Analysis of "St. Paul."

DURING all this activity in Mendelssohn's external
life, his productive talent was no less eagerly
engaged. His great oratorio of "St. Paul," begun in
Düsseldorf, was finished at Leipzig during the course of
this winter. The author seems to have been bound by
a promise to produce this work at a musical festival of
Lower-Rhine artists, to be held at Düsseldorf. At any
rate, the chorus-parts were engraved at Bonn by Simrock, after the piece was completed, and sent to Düsseldorf. Under the direction of Julius Rietz, the rehearsals
were carried on with great enthusiasm; and when, on
the 8th of May, 1836, Mendelssohn arrived in person,
he found the work all ready for the public performance.
On Whitsunday, the 22d of May, occurred the introduction of the oratorio of "St. Paul" to the world. The
solos were Madame Fischer-Achten, Miss Grabau (now

Madame Bünau), Messieurs Schmetzer and Wersing,
the latter as St. Paul. As a curious fact, it may
be remarked, that the two false witnesses in the unim-
portant duet at the opening, "We have heard him
utter blasphemies," could not find their voices when
their turn came to sing. The success of the piece was
decidedly brilliant. Mendelssohn's sister, herself only
and hardly second to her brother in musical genius, —
Fanny Hensel, whose tragic death her brother Felix
was soon called to deplore, — and the younger brother,
Paul Mendelssohn, had come from Berlin to be present
at the first performance of "St. Paul." On the second
day of the festival, Beethoven's "Ninth Symphony," and
the first overture to "Leonora," then freshly produced,
Mozart's "Davidde Penitente," and a great psalm in E
flat, by Handel. On the third day, Mendelssohn played,
with Ferdinand David, the great "A-minor Sonata" of
Beethoven; and as the music was not at hand, and this
piece had not been specially indicated for the occasion,
he played from memory. The Committee of Direction
signified their gratification at Mendelssohn's signal success by presenting him with a magnificent copy of the
oratorio of "St. Paul," adorned with elegant drawings
of the leading scenes in the sacred drama, executed by
the first artists of Düsseldorf, — Schrötter, Hübner,
Steinbrück, Mücke; to which one was added by Mendelssohn's brother-in-law, the court-painter Hensel.

After the first representation of " St. Paul," Mendelssohn made so many and so great changes in the work, that the great number of voices was unnecessary. Ten pieces he left entirely out; and the first great aria in B minor, he reduced to about a third of its original length. On the other hand, he composed, some days before the festival, the short soprano solo in F major, in the second part; not to speak of innumerable smaller changes in the body of the work.

After this festival was past, Mendelssohn went to Frankfort-on-the-Main, in order to direct at the public celebration of the " Cecilia" (*Cäcilien - Verein*) in the place of his friend Schelble, who had been very ill, and was trying the restorative effect of sea-bathing. This society afforded great delight to Mendelssohn, in consequence of its large number of fine voices, and the secure mastery which it had acquired of the most difficult motets of Sebastian Bach. The city and suburbs of Frankfort, which he had seen and known only as a child, or when he flitted through it on his journeys, pleased him exceedingly. He enjoyed himself so well there, that he has left on record, in a sportive letter, that, if he should stay much longer in Frankfort, he should certainly become a devoted gardener. During his cheerful occupations there, he discovered one blossom so fair, that he took it to himself, to adorn the garden of his whole future life. He was introduced by a friend to the

4

Jeanrenaud Family, and there made the acquaintance
of the youngest daughter, Cecilia, who afterwards became his wife. When the nuptial band united them,
there was no one who thought that it was so soon to be
sundered. She was worthy of such a husband; and she
showed it not only through their whole married life, but
most of all by the heroic fortitude with which she bore
her loss.*

On the advice of his physician at Leipzig, Mendelssohn took a journey to Scheveningen, after his duties
at Frankfort were concluded, in order to enjoy a course
of sea-bathing. There he remained for some time; and
with nerves much strengthened, and his general health
improved, he turned back, in the autumn of the same
year (1836), to renew his work at Leipzig. On the
2d of October, we see him re-instated in his old place
as director of the concerts at the Gewandhaus. He
opened them with that overture to " Leonora " which we
have just seen was brought out at the Düsseldorf Festival; which was soon repeated at an extra concert given
by Lipinski, with the finale from Cherubini's " Water-
carrier," " O God! my eye deceives me not," and Beethoven's "A-major Symphony." Besides this, Mademoiselle
Grabau sang an aria, with chorus, from Mercadante;
and David played a new concertino of his own composition. A number of pieces, the chief of which was the

* She died in September, 1853.

"A-major Symphony," were given with great applause. At the second subscription concert, at repeated request, Beethoven's "Heroic Symphony" was given. It was, as we learn from an account written at the time, played in the most faultless manner, in one spirit from the first note to the last; and this master-work of the greatest of masters left nothing that could be wished. It was applauded at the end of every movement, and its delicious tones echoed in the memory long after the piece was ended. At the third concert, a symphony in B major was brought out, one of the genial Haydn's; and at the fourth was played that royal second overture to "Leonora" (with the flourish of trumpets), and so finely, that not only was the applause unusually hearty and sustained, but the whole piece had to be played from first to last; an honor not often showed in that hall. In these concerts there was sometimes given, as is now often the case, a new symphony, carefully studied, by some living composer. At the concert of which I write, it was the "Sinfonia Appassionata" (so successful in Vienna), by Franz Lachner.

Meanwhile, there was an admirable opportunity in Leipzig to learn the marvellous power of Mendelssohn as a leader, and to test at the same time the extent of musical resources in that art-loving city. "Israel in Egypt," that master-piece of Handel's, whose great effects are in the chorus parts, was studied. Upon these

choruses Mendelssohn began to work, having rehearsal
follow rehearsal with great rapidity; and, as the singers
were promptness and loyalty itself, he soon wove the
most discordant elements into unity, and brought about
a very perfect result. He did a good service in other
respects; for he wrote out in full notes Handel's figured
organ bass, which is not read with ease by organists
of our day. On Nov. 7, 1836, it was magnificently
brought out in St. Paul's Church, with a chorus of more
than two hundred and fifty voices, assisted by the organ
and a strong orchestra. The success of the oratorio
well repaid the patient care and skill of preparation.
The great interest in the work was manifested by the
immense audience which filled the spacious church.
Thus Leipzig celebrated its first great Musical Festival,
and with no common splendor.

Of the other musical performances and concerts of
this winter when Mendelssohn was the conductor, and
which were therefore directed with matchless skill, I
will refer to only one. It was the last concert of 1836,
and took place on the 12th of December. It was to
have been on Thursday; but out of love to Mendelssohn,
and out of regard to his yearning after Frankfort, it
was given on the preceding Monday. After Mendelssohn had played, with rare skill, Beethoven's " E-flat
Major Concerto " for the first part, and closed in a storm
of applause, the second part opened with his own " A

Calm at Sea, and a Happy Voyage;" then followed some solo performances, and then the happily chosen finale of "Fidelio." The reader will remember that the great chorus of "Fidelio" has the words, —

> "Whoe'er a lovely bride has won,
> Let him now join our gladsome song."

Mendelssohn, being called to the piano by the repeated applause which followed this chorus, seated himself, and began to extemporize on the theme, working it up in the most brilliant manner. It seemed like a great family party, to which he had invited the guests to share in his own private joy. Every one who had a heart rejoiced with him. All knew what his errand to Frankfort was.

It is also worthy of remark, that, this same winter, a friend of Mendelssohn, remarkable both for his performances on the piano and also for his own compositions, visited Germany, and awakened much enthusiasm by his brilliant talents. William Sterndale Bennett had come from England in order to study musical composition under Mendelssohn for a season. He displayed the value of the instructions he received in a delightful piano-forte concerto in C minor, and also in a very attractive overture, written in Mendelssohn's manner, but still pleasantly remembered. Later, we heard from the young composer a second overture, "The Wood Nymph," which was one of the most charming pictures of natural scenery ever presented, and captivated all hearers. And, lastly, it may be remarked, that, at the last subscription concert of this season, Beethoven's grand "Ninth Symphony" was given, even more perfectly, if possible, than at its first performance.

And now had come the time when the tried and proved musical resources of Leipzig could be fitly put to a fine test of their reach and compass; and that was on the occasion of bringing out Mendelssohn's oratorio of "St. Paul," now widely known, and in many countries. The chorus began their rehearsals in February, 1837; and every thing that the director's skill, zeal, and thoroughness could accomplish was done, and all that the thorough co-operation of the singers could effect was conjoined with even greater spirit and willingness than at the representation of Handel's "Israel in Egypt." The noble choruses and chorals, although accompanied merely by a wretched piano, wrought powerfully upon the choir, and, despite the repeated necessary rehearsals, raised public expectation to its height. Most impressive of all were the choral, "Awake! the Voice calls," whose imposing effect, with the trombone accompaniment, could only be conjectured when sung to the piano; the sublime chorus, "Arise! the light breaks, thy light comes;" and the voice from heaven, in the blended soprano and alto, "Saul, Saul, why persecutest thou me?" But scarcely less effective and moving were all those passages which bear the stamp of a Christian's joy, of pious self-renunciation, and untroubled confidence : as, for example, that first chorus, which rang out like a pæan of victory, " Lord, thou art God, who hast made heaven and earth;" that choral, full of inward humility and the love of God, " To thee, O God! will I commit myself;" and those two precious, sadly joyous choruses, " Behold, we count them happy that endure," and " The Lord will wipe away all tears from their eyes, for he hath spoken it;" the first of which, with its swelling waves of sound and its wonderful power, moved every heart to its depths. There was not in the whole oratorio a single chorus which we did not take delight in singing; and Mendelssohn understood, as hardly any other director has equally done, how to make his singers sing with their whole souls. This appeared in the perfect execution of the pianos, only breathed out; the crescendos and diminuendos, whose possibilities, significance, and effect he first revealed to us.

After such thorough drill, not only in the choruses, but in the solo and the orchestral parts, the public performance of the work, which took place on the 16th of March, 1837, could not fail to be successful in the highest degree. It was a disappointment that the bass soloist, who was to take the part of St. Paul, was obliged to be absent in consequence of illness ; but the gentleman who took his place sustained the part well. In the recitative, Mademoisclle Grabau was especially excellent. I do not remember who the other soloists were. The choir consisted of over three hundred voices, with a correspondingly large orchestra. I must let another speak for me regarding the general effect; for I was one of the performers on the occasion. The critic of the "Musical Gazette" says, "Under the skilful leading of the composer, the great orchestra did its work masterly; and the choruses, already thoroughly studied under Director Dr. Mendelssohn Bartholdy, were given in noble style, so bright, powerful, full, round, and shaded to every nicety of expression, that I never saw the effect in so large a choir equalled. Whoever was present at the representation of that brilliant work will be compelled to confess, that the larger share of the credit which the choir gained for itself is owing to the matchless skill of the conductor and the power of the piece itself. With simple justice has the management of the subscription concerts offered its public thanks to the honored leader, the soloists, the orchestra, its conductor David, and the entire body of singers, for their unwearied patience in preparation, and their brilliant performance on the night of representation."

To enter on a close and critical analysis of a work which has made the circuit of the civilized world, and has everywhere received recognition as a great work of

art, is not in place here: it does not come within my
domain as Mendelssohn's biographer. Only some ex-
planatory remarks are suitable here. From a strictly
æsthetical point of view, the " St. Paul " may have many
defects. Unquestionably, the personal agency of Paul
at the martyrdom of Stephen is kept somewhat in the
background; and the second part of the oratorio is
inferior to the first in dramatic interest. But the main
thought which runs through the whole work is too high
and broad to be linked by the tie of a personal interest
to any single man: it is the glorification of Christianity,
with its humility, its joy in living and dying for the
Lord, in contrast with the blind self-righteousness of
Judaism, and the mere sensuous morality of the Heathen
schools; it is the contrast, or rather the struggle, of
the last two with the former, and the victory of the
light and love of the gospel,—the light eternal, the love
divine. This thought is made incarnate in the persons
of Stephen, Paul, and Barnabas; and it is concentrated
at that point which is really the central point of interest to the oratorio,—the conversion of St. Paul. Mendelssohn has been reproached because he represented
the voice of the Lord by a choir of women's voices, or
angels perhaps: it would have been better, they say, if
simulated by a powerful blast on the trombone. But
that very golden mean between the sharp distinctness
of a man's voice and the inarticulate sound of a mere

instrument seems to me a masterly conception of the
composer; for it transcends the common, the expected,
and becomes, to say the least, unique; if not supernatu-
ral, yet not unreasonable. Nor does this objection hold
good in point of fact; for no one who ever heard the
oratorio has failed to notice the striking effect of those
female voices on every hearer of susceptibility. Upon
whom has that sound not broken like the very voice of
the presence of God? And how solemnly deep becomes
the impression at the massive chorus, "Arise! the light
is breaking!" which cleaves the darkness like a thunder-
bolt from heaven! What an impressive warning to
change his ways in the statuesque choral which follows,
"Awake! the voice doth call!" and what a pæan of victory to come in that majestic passage, the trombone
accompanying every line, which declares the glory of
the ancient Zion, new glorified by the light of the later
dispensation! How powerful the contrast in the choruses of the Christian, the Jewish, and the Pagan
faiths! Compare only the chorus, "Behold, we count
them happy which endure," and "Oh the depth of the
riches of the wisdom and the knowledge of God!" with
the chorus of Jews, "This man ceases not to utter blas-
phemy;" and, "Here is the Lord's temple! — ye men
of Israel, help;" and these again with the choruses,
"The gods have come to us in the likeness of men;" and,
"Be gracious to us, ye gods," — and you will not fail to

see how sharply delineated and discriminated are these three faiths. A peculiar, and at the same time a beautiful feature of the oratorio is given by the chorals, which are always so suitably introduced to add solemnity, and yet a kindly grace, to the work. They give a truly Christian character to the whole; yet the effect of those perfect pieces of harmony is subduing and soothing. Doubtless there are many to whom church music is a novelty, so to speak, who hear these chorals, and wonder that strains so sweet and elevating are sung all around them, and have remained unknown to them. It may be that this musical effect is largely to be ascribed to the great Bach; but does the composer who a hundred years later restores the Christian choral, with its depth of feeling and tender spirituality, with the attractions of modern art, deserve less praise? Lastly, it is impossible to overrate the skill with which the great author has united words, taken only from the Bible, into a round and full historical painting, and has thus solved one of the greatest practical difficulties. And although, in my opinion, the chief attractions of this oratorio lie in the choruses and chorals, yet there is no lack of merit in the solos. The recitatives are beautifully distinct; and the two arias of Paul, the passage, "Destroy them, Lord God of Sabaoth," and the penitential strain, "God be gracious to me according to thy loving-kindness," could not more finely combine dramatic effect with strict adherence to the church style. Again, in the soprano aria, " Jerusalem, thou that killest the prophets; " in the arioso for the alto, " Yet the Lord is mindful of his own; " in the aria of Paul, " I thank thee, O Lord ! " — no one will fail to see the union of the truest Christian feeling with the most artistic musical form. The whole oratorio is, in one word, *edifying,* and that in the deepest sense : it strengthens, it exalts, it ennobles the spirit by its happy combination of religious sentiment with noble harmony. Where the eternally *true* and the eternally *beautiful* lock hands together, there is the highest consummation of all possible excellences that art can furnish, and there must be the happiest results.

CHAPTER VI.

ADORNED with the fresh laurel-wreath which the production of "St. Paul" in Leipzig had won for him, and not figuratively merely, but literally, — for a laurel wreath was laid upon his music-stand by admiring friends, — Mendelssohn hurried to Frankfort to blend the laurel of fame with the myrtle of love.   In the spring of 1837, his union with Cecilia Jeanrenaud, the second daughter of a deceased clergyman of Dresden, was solemnly celebrated.   "Ah! those were pleasant days."   In August of the same year, in company with his bride, whose beauty and amiability made a universally favorable impression, he visited his old friends in Düsseldorf, with whom, with the exception of Immermann, he remained on terms of the greatest cordiality. He was very fond of Düsseldorf.   He himself confessed that his visits to that place were among the happiest events of his life.   He was always on the move, was in the brightest spirits, and gratified all wishes to hear him

play, weary as it might make him. Here, to please
and honor him, " St. Paul " was brought out under the
direction of his pupil and friend, Rietz. He himself
could show to his friends, as the fruit of his recent activity, the forty-second Psalm (Op. 42), a new piano concerto with orchestral accompaniment in D minor (Op.
40), and the violin quartet in E minor (Op. 44, No. 2),
all in manuscript. The bright days after his marriage
had not interfered with his productive power, nor dimin-
ished the affluent gifts of his genius. From Düsseldorf
he sent to Simrock at Bonn, all ready for the press,
the three motets for women's voices, partly composed
at Rome. From Düsseldorf he went, without his wife,
over to England, where he was expected to direct the
bringing-out of " St. Paul " at the great Musical Festival
at Birmingham from the 19th to the 22d of September. The oratorio was given the second day, in the
presence of an immense concourse of hearers, but with
some omissions in the second part. The work was received with the greatest favor: the choruses were sung
with unrivalled power, though not always carefully
enough. Mendelssohn's appearance in the orchestra,
towards the end of the piece, was greeted with a storm
of applause. In September of the same year, " St.
Paul " was produced for the first time at Berlin.

On his return from England, we see Mendelssohn
take his wonted place as director of the concerts given

ın the Gewandhaus, and received, at his first appearance in public, with a very kindly greeting. The Jubilee overture by Weber, a chorus by Haydn, Beethoven's C-minor symphony, the song from "The Freischütz," "Wie nahte mir der Schlummer," sung by Louise Schlegel (a very gifted pupil of Director Pohlenz), and a new concerto composed and played by David, opened the series of winter entertainments in a most excellent and attractive manner. It would weary the reader were I to enter into a full specification of the performances of that winter, any further than as they were connected with Mendelssohn himself. One excellent fruit of his visit to England, so far as Germany is concerned, was the visit of an extremely talented, cultivated, and prepossessing artiste, — Miss Clara Novello; who, however, sang but seven times in Leipzig, but left us filled with regret at her too-speedy departure. She was the daughter of a music-publisher in London, for whom, as early as 1832, Mendelssohn had composed a "Morning Service." Her bell-like, silver voice, her perfect training, and her charming appearance, won all hearts. The concerts were more crowded than ever. She made her first appearance at the fifth subscription concert, in the arias, "Ecco il punto, O Vitellia!" from "Titus," and "Casta Diva" from "Norma;" and, at her last appearance, she sang Beethoven's great scena, "Abscheulicher! wo eilst du hin?" At the third subscription concert, Mendelssohn played his new piano-concerto in D minor ("Allegro appassionato, Adagio, and Scherzo giojoso," as he then called the closing passage), and, of course, won the most enthusiastic applause. At the second quartet entertainment, Mendelssohn produced a new quartet, — the one in E minor (Op. 44) which he had taken to Düsseldorf; and the second and last movements were received with special favor. The second was encored. At the concert in behalf of poor and sick musicians, the overture to the "Midsummer Night's Dream" was given, and Mendelssohn himself played his "Capriccio brillant" in B minor (Op. 22). During all this varied round of activities, he yet found time to bring together the musical resources of Leipzig for the purpose of producing one of the great master-pieces of the past. After repeated rehearsals, Handel's "Messiah" was given at St. Paul's Church. The number of singers in the choruses was equal to that on former similar occasions. The solos were sustained by artists of the highest excellence. This master-piece was rendered according to Mozart's arrangement; and in several passages rather choral-like, and at the close of certain choruses, the effect was heightened by the full organ accompaniment. The performance of the choir, soloists, and orchestra, was one of the finest ever witnessed; and the impression left by the whole work was wholly satisfactory.

The year 1838 brought to light another product of Mendelssohn's Muse. The music of the forty-second Psalm, which he had shown to his Düsseldorf friends, was sung for the first time in public at the tenth subscription concert, and displayed at once the character of a wholly unique and artistic work. Never has the soul's inmost yearning after God been spoken out in tones more searching and tender. After the chorus has uttered this passionate longing in those noble words, so grandly set to music in this piece, " As the hart pants after the water-brooks, so panteth my soul for thee, O God!" a delicate soprano solo, " For my soul thirsteth," takes up a slow strain full of the inmost tenderness of longing. Then follows a chorus of women's voices, justifying, as it were, her who has just sung, and giving more express utterance to what all feel in the words, " For I had gone with the multitude ; I went with them to the house of God,"— a passage which, by its march-movement, suggests a light-hearted walk to the temple of God. Then comes a chorus of men's voices, uttering words both of admonition and consolation: " Why art thou cast down, O my soul? hope thou in God." But that first plaintive woman's cry, justifying its very wail by its eager desire to enjoy the presence of God, is heard in yet sharper and distincter tones: " O my God! my soul is cast down within me : all thy waves and thy billows are gone over me." Then strikes

5

in, accompanied by stringed instruments, a noble quartet of men's voices, full of consolation and truthful faith : " Yet the Lord will command his loving-kindness in the day-time ; and in the night his song shall be with me, and my prayer unto the God of my life." Yet with their voices still mingles that plaintive soprano strain, almost wailing, in its extreme sadness ; till, at the end, the whole choir of men and women take up the opening passage again with the full confidence of belief and hope in God, and close with an ascription of praise to the Lord God of Israel. The whole makes a brief but complete religious tone-drama, as it may be called. Yet those who have not heard Mendelssohn's music of the forty-second Psalm cannot imagine how beautiful it is from this imperfect sketch : it is rather for those who may by its help call back in memory pleasures which they have enjoyed before in listening to its wondrous harmony. And these will confess that not easily can a smoother and more pleasing movement, musical expression better adapted to words, and nobler melodies, be found, than are combined in this composition. The first performance, particularly the choruses and the soprano part, sustained by Miss Novello, was admirable.

Later in the course of these concerts, some interesting new symphonies were given, and another less generally attractive Psalm of Mendelssohn, written earlier, — the hundred and fifteenth.* Mendelssohn's next great step was to propose a series of concerts, indicating the historical development of music. On the 15th of February, they were opened with a selection from the works of Sebastian Bach, Handel, Gluck, and Viotti. After a suite by Bach, followed Handel's hymn, " Great is the Lord ; " then a sonata in E major (No. 3) for piano-forte and violin, played by Mendelssohn and David. The second part was made up of the overture, introduction, and first scene of the " Iphigenia in Tauris," by Gluck ; followed by a concerto for the violin, from Viotti, played exceedingly well by David. The second of these concerts was from the works of Haydn, Cimarosa, Naumann, and Righini. The programme of this concert is too interesting to be wholly excluded from these pages : overture to " Tigranes," and aria from " Armida," by Righini ; overture to Cimarosa's " Matrimonio Segreto ; " trio by Haydn for piano, violin, and violoncello (C major), played by Mendelssohn, David, and Grenser ; introduction, recitative, and closing scena of the first part of Haydn's " Creation." The second part was composed of a quintet and chorus from " I Pellegrini " by Naumann, and the " Parting " symphony by Haydn. The third of these concerts was made up of selections from Mozart, Salieri,

* In the concert for the poor, given Feb. 21, 1838, the ninety-fifth Psalm, with Mendelssohn's music, was given for the first time; an excellent piece, sung with full chorus.

Méhul, and Andreas Romberg; among other things, a hitherto wholly unknown quartet from Mozart's "Zaida," and an ensemble from Méhul's "Uthal," an opera, which the author had composed, at Napoleon's command, from a subject in " Ossian," and entirely without violins. The shining feature of this concert was a piano-forte concerto by Mozart in C minor, played by Mendelssohn. The overture to the " Magic Flute" was also exceedingly well given. The programme of the fourth of these concerts was selected from Vogler, Beethoven, and Von Weber. The overture to Vogler's " Samori," overture to Weber's "Freischütz," and the hunters' chorus from " Euryanthe," Beethoven's great " Violin Concerto" and the " Pastoral Symphony," were the most striking features of this evening's entertainment, which brought this course of historical concerts to a worthy close. That they not only awakened in the public an interest in the history of music, but also largely promoted a genuine musical taste among the Leipzig people, needs hardly be said.

Thus, through Mendelssohn's efforts mainly, the winter was passed in the enjoyment of the richest treasures which music could afford the people of that art-loving city which was his home. During the next summer, he enjoyed no rest. He went again to the Rhine, — this time to assume the direction of the Cologne Musical Festival. The "Joshua" of Handel was selected as the chief piece; and for this, as he had done for the

" Solomon" before, he resorted to the organ as a leading auxiliary. The whole festival was most brilliant. The separation from his wife seemed to be a great trial to Mendelssohn. He was somewhat sad; but yet, on the third day, he played his " Serenade and Allegro gio-joso." His true friend and fellow-artist, David, accompanied him to the Rhine.

No sooner had he returned to Leipzig, than the liveliest wish was expressed on all sides that the " St. Paul " should be repeated. Mendelssohn showed a willingness to comply with the general desire, and conducted the rehearsals with his accustomed care. But, when the day of the public performance arrived, — the 15th of September, 1838, — Mendelssohn himself was unable to be present; being attacked by the measles. David was compelled to take his place; and he conducted so much in the spirit of the great author of the work, that the effect was even deeper on some hearers than it had been the first time. It is to be mentioned, that after the choral, No. 9, " To thee, O Lord! do I commit myself," a new alto aria had been introduced, — " Thou who bring-est us to destruction, and sayest, Return, ye children of men." The leading soprano solos this time were sustained by a very lovely singer, who, though now occupying a high position in distinguished society, still continued to dedicate her remarkable gifts to the art of music, especially to the Muse of Mendelssohn; and who remains his best interpreter to this day. After this representation of " Paulus," a number took place in Leipzig, the last of which was directed by the author, and occurred on Good Friday, 1847. No other great musical work has ever gained such speedy recognition as the " St. Paul." In the history of music, the years 1837 and 1838 might be called the "St. Paul" years. A computation has been attempted of the number of places where this oratorio was sung within a year and a half, and the number of times it was sung; and it was found to be not less than fifty times in forty-one different cities. In Germany, in Poland, in Russia, in the Tyrol and Switzerland, in Denmark, in Holland, in England, in America, everywhere, " St. Paul " was given, and in some places two or three times.

CHAPTER VII.

The Leipzig Concerts. — Mrs. Alfred Shaw. — A memorable Musical Winter. — Mendelssohn conducts the Spring Festival at Düsseldorf. — The next Winter's Concerts. — The Hundred and Fourteenth Psalm: its Musical Effects. — New Instrumental Music.

THE time for the author of a piece held in such estimation to be taken away had not yet come. Providence watched over him: he soon recovered from his sickness. The direction of the first subscription concert was left to his friend David; but at the second we find Mendelssohn in his old place, more a favorite than ever, and received with the greatest joy. He opened this concert with his overture to " Fingal's Cave." In the third concert, after the enthusiastically received and encored overture to the " Freischütz," an English singer appeared, for whose advent in Leipzig we were indebted to Mendelssohn, — Mrs. Alfred Shaw, a lady of imposing figure, endowed with a remarkably clear and full voice. The noble simplicity of her style, and her thorough conception of the subject, particularly in songs of deep feeling, made her appearance before a Leipzig audience very acceptable. She sang first a recitative and an aria by Rossini, " Amici, in ogni evento m'affido a voi," and the

"Addio" of Mozart. Her stay till the 28th of January gave us a continual round of enjoyments. In the most tender and touching manner she sang the aria from Handel's "Messiah," "He was despised and rejected of men;" and indeed her selection of subjects was always the happiest possible. But this circumstance arose primarily from the admirable works chosen by Mendelssohn as the basis for the concerts. The reader who goes over the programme of that winter's entertainments is astonished at the wealth of classic pieces, and their tasteful collocation in relation to each other. Handel, Gluck, Haydn, Beethoven, Mozart, Cherubini, Weber, Spohr, Rossini, alternate in the list, yet not to the exclusion of the later and the latest masters in music. For example, new symphonies by Kalliwoda, Lachner, Möhring, and Dobrycinski were given, and the newly discovered symphony by Franz Schubert (C major), which took the palm from all the rest. As an example of a genuine classic programme, which yet did not lack the charm of the greatest variety, take this one: overture to "Iphigenia," by Gluck; chorus, "The dust's vain cares," by Haydn; "O salutaris hostia!" by Cherubini, sung by Mrs. Shaw; variations for the violin, by Lipinski, played by Ulrich; cavatina from "Romeo and Juliet," by Zingarelli, sung by Mrs. Shaw; symphony in A major, by Beethoven. Although the power of selecting lay in the management, yet it was really Mendelssohn's judgment that controlled the decision. As a special advantage of these concerts, may be mentioned this, — that a great number of fine pieces, from operas which were unfortunately almost neglected on the stage, were thus brought into notice; for instance, the delightful sextet from "Cosi fan Tutte," the trio with chorus from "Medea," the Polonaise, trio, and chorus from Cherubini's "Lodoiska." Sometimes they were taken from well-known, excellent operas; for instance, the first finale from "Euryanthe," the trio and quartet from "Oberon," the aria and first finale from the same, and the second finale from "Leonora."

From Mendelssohn there were given this winter the overtures, "Fingal's Cave," and "A Calm at Sea and Happy Voyage;" the overture to "St. Paul," with the recitative and aria from the same oratorio, "And he drew with the throng towards Damascus" (given at the New-Year's concert, together with Beethoven's C-minor Symphony); an overture to "Ruy Blas;" and the Forty-second Psalm, — the last two at the twentieth subscription concert, when Schubert's symphony in C major, and the "Spring" from Haydn's "Seasons," were brought out for the first time.

In the spring of 1839, Mendelssohn, in conjunction with Julius Rietz, conducted the Düsseldorf Festival. A combination of distinguished singers, such as Fassmann, Clara Novello, &c., made this festival one of the most brilliant ever known. Handel's "Messiah," and Beethoven's Mass in C, were given as the chief pieces. Here Mendelssohn first became acquainted with Sophia Schloss, who so finely sustained the alto solos in the "Messiah" and the Mass of Beethoven, that he engaged her for the next winter at Leipzig. Of Mendelssohn's own works, the Forty-second Psalm was given. On the third day of the festival, he played his D-minor Concerto, and accompanied many songs on the pianoforte.

In the winter of 1839 and 1840, he again directed the Leipzig concerts, with the same care and the same success which had been so marked in the previous winter. Besides Sophia Schloss, Eliza Meerti was engaged, a Belgian lady, who united a solid style and an agreeable voice with French ease and elegance. A number of new gifts from Mendelssohn's Muse delighted us that winter, besides the treasures of past time. The concert in celebration of the great Reformation, given on Wednesday, the 30th of October, 1839, was opened with a new adaptation to music, by Mendelssohn, of Luther's hymn, "In mercy grant us peace, O Lord!" The purest and deepest spirituality which can accompany prayer is the character of this noble piece, as Mendelssohn gave it to the world. Had this music, as well as that written to Luther's noble hymn, "In the midst of life," appeared in Rome, we should have seen

in it, not a simple fortuitous circumstance, but the rise
of a true Protestant spirit (not indeed in the ordinary
use of language), — a spirit of protest against the mere
sensuous coloring which the Catholic Church gives to
all its ideas, as well as to its worship. But, whether on
purpose or accidentally, the authorship of the piece was
not avowed at the concert. If the taste of the musical
public were to be put to the test, it might be said that it
has not yet showed that it was always united on any
point, — not thoroughly at one, so to speak, — as to any
piece; and this production of Mendelssohn's was quietly,
not to say coolly, received. Perhaps it was in consequence of the deeply religious character of the piece;
this kind of music does not usually win much out-
ward demonstration from a Leipzig audience; but so
much is certain, — the authorship of the piece was then
unknown, except to the initiated few.

It ought not to be passed by without mention, that on
the 25th of December, in the same year, " St. Paul "
was brought out in Munich for the first time. It made
the same deep impression as everywhere.

The year 1840, one of the most fruitful in its addi-
tions to Mendelssohn's well-merited and always ascend-
ing fame, gave us as the first-fruits of his genius a new
and great production. It was the Hundred and fourteenth Psalm, " When Israel out of Egypt came," which
he composed for full chorus and orchestra. It was given

for the first time at the New-Year's concert; and although in character and treatment wholly different from the Forty-second Psalm, yet, in its way, it is almost as great. The selection of this Psalm, one of the finest, if not the very finest, of Old-Testament lyrics, was a very happy conception of the composer; and how skilfully has he brought out in music the praise and the majesty of God! In one great flood of inspiration, peaceful, and yet overpowering, the double chorus strikes in, " What ailed thee, O thou sea! that thou fleddest? — thou Jordan, that thou wast driven back? " With the greatest sublimity the answer comes back, " Tremble, thou earth, at the presence of the Lord; " and the whole widens at the close into the grand fugue, " Hallelujah! sing to the Lord," which seems like the very ocean of eternity. Let the reader imagine to himself one of those psalms of the temple, in which the choir, accompanied by the trombones of the Levites, announced the glory of the Lord from the holy place, accompanied by all the helps of contemporaneous art, and in the most spiritual (i.e., the least sensuous) form, and he has a conception of the effect of this masterpiece, in which the musical expression is perfectly adapted to every word; and yet the whole stream of sound flows in a single channel.

In an entirely different domain of his art was the third great work which the unwearied genius of Mendelssohn gave us that winter. It was the charming trio in D minor for piano-forte, violin, and violoncello (Op. 49), first played in public by himself, David, and Witt-mann, the 1st of February of that year. This piece expressed in its first strain that ardent feeling, that almost passionate power, which was more especially the mark of Mendelssohn's genius than of any modern artist. The andante con moto tranquillo, which follows, is filled with that equally inimitable longing and sub-dued and plaintive joy. The scherzo plays with the charm of infantile grace; while the finale, in its allegro assai appassionato, satisfies and charms the ear with its strong tones and balanced rhythm. The whole work is a true mirror of Mendelssohn in his most spiritual-minded and deepest mood, a product of one of the happi-est hours of his genius, uttering itself in perfect frank-ness and the most artistic form. It was received, of course, with the greatest applause.

It would be easy to recall and to speak with enthu-siasm of many other musical enjoyments of that winter, which we owe to Mendelssohn. But I will, out of regard to the reader, confine myself to the most impor-tant; and simply record, that, on the 9th of January, all the four overtures to Beethoven's " Fidelio " were given under Mendelssohn's direction. It was a matter of interest to every friend of art to follow this great-est of all masters into the secret chambers of his genius, and to see, as perhaps he had never before done, the greatness of the work, the majesty of the conception; and in no better way could he do this than under the guidance of an artist of kindred genius, and of equal ambition. And it was a proof of the thorough training of our Leipzig musical public, that these four overtures were not received with simple satisfaction, but were thoroughly enjoyed.

Of the first appearance of Liszt in Leipzig, which occurred in January of this year, and in which Mendelssohn had an honorable part in introducing him to favorable notice, I shall speak more fully in another place. Let me only remark here, that during that same month, Fétis, at the first concert of the Conservatoire in Brussels, brought out, in conjunction with Beethoven's "Heroic Symphony" and the overture to Cherubini's "Anacreon," the overture to the "Midsummer Night's Dream," which wrought an immediate and powerful impression on the audience.

CHAPTER VIII.

The " Hymn of Praise." — Its Occasion, History, first Performance, Musical
Character, and remarkable Success.

WE now arrive at a point in the career of Mendelssohn which was signalized by the production,
and public performance under his own direction, of
what must be considered, if not his greatest work, at
least his most genial one, and the one which indicated
the meridian splendor of his career. The occasion which
called it forth was the fourth centennial celebration
of the invention of printing, which, though observed
with great demonstrations of respect throughout all the
larger cities of Germany, was especially honored in
Leipzig, — the place which had been built up by the new
art, as it were; at any rate, whose reputation as the
birthplace of books was identified with the history of
printing. It was a theme of general rejoicing, that the
care of the musical part was given into Mendelssohn's
hands; and no one could fail to see that he entered upon
the execution of this trust with eager hope. The first
task was to procure a hymn which should be the text,
as it were, for Mendelssohn's music, to be sung at the

www.ingramcontent.com/pod-product-compliance
Lightning Source LLC
Chambersburg PA
CBHW032356020726
47499CB00008B/2777